Rabbit and the Well

Rabbit and the Well

Story by **Deborah L. Duvall**

Paintings by **Murv Jacob**

University of New Mexico Press ⬤ Albuquerque

To Our Brothers and Sisters:
Merrill, Spyder, Mike, Roger, Neicey, and Jeannie

Artist's Note: The great storyteller Joel Chandler Harris had his narrative character, Uncle Remus, tell an antebellum version of this story that he called "The Tar Baby." Harris remained sure to his life's end that the stories he collected of Brer Rabbit, Brer Bear, Brer Fox, and the others were derived from African folk legends.

My closest Cherokee cultural informants, the likes of Cecil Dick, Pat Moss, and Robert J. Conley, convinced me years ago that this story is from the Cherokee cycle of animal tales that has evolved since times ancient right here on ol' Turtle Island. I would note that the wise and very human animal characters in both versions of the story are all New World species; they are not lions, elephants, or monkeys—the typical African animals you would expect to find in folk stories carried to America from Africa. As to the cultural diversity, I'll let you readers ponder that whilst comparing the two.

In the late decades of the 1800s, while Harris was crafting his "Tar Baby" tale in the red hills of Georgia, the noted ethnographer James Mooney was collecting the Cherokee story variants not that far north on the Cherokee Reservation of North Carolina's Smoky Mountains, and also here in Indian Territory. Duvall's new version rings with the great old Cherokee attitude of community spirit and selfless involvement to achieve necessary goals.

M. Jacob

13 12 11 10 09 08   1 2 3 4 5 6 7

Library of Congress Cataloging-in-Publication Data

Duvall, Deborah L., 1952–
  Rabbit and the well / story by Deborah L. Duvall ; drawings by Murv Jacob.
    p. cm.
  ISBN 978-0-8263-4331-4 (cloth : alk. paper)
  1. Rabbit (Legendary character) 2. Cherokee Indians—Folklore. 3. Tales—Great Plains.
  I. Jacob, Murv, ill. II. Title.
    E99.C5D8943 2008
    398.20978—dc22
                        2007031865

BOOK DESIGN AND TYPE COMPOSITION BY MELISSA TANDYSH ❋
COMPOSED IN 14/23 ITC CHELTENHAM STD LIGHT ❋ DISPLAY TYPE IS SASSAFRAS STD ❋
PRINTED ON 150 GSM GRYCKSBO MATT ❋ BOUND IN SAIFU CLOTH ❋
PRINTED AND BOUND IN SINGAPORE BY TWP AMERICA

Rabbit, whose name in Cherokee is Ji-Stu, stared up into the sky, sweeping his eyes from the east to the west.

He hoped today he would see one—a rain cloud. He looked out toward the river that ran past his house in the broom grass meadow.

"Surely the Long Man has never been this small," Ji-Stu said, using the name for the river that his old uncle taught him.

Ji-Stu looked across the narrow stream at his home. The river once filled those empty banks that now stretched far away from the shore. Ji-Stu had stopped using his canoe weeks ago. Why, he could easily jump across the river now!

More weeks passed, and the river and all the other bodies of water near the great forest where Ji-Stu the Rabbit lived began to dry up. The animals called a council and made plans to save as much of the precious water as possible.

"We should dam up the river," said Beaver, the famous dam builder, who jumped up to speak as the animal council began. "I'll do the work myself!"

"Wa-do, thank you, Beaver," Terrapin the Doctor said. "But we must not disturb the river's path, because the Long Man knows where he is going and the best way to get there."

"We could store the water in pots made of clay," suggested Raccoon, waving her nimble fingers in the air. "And those of us with hands can make them!"

Everyone in the council agreed that Raccoon's idea was best. So three more with hands, Si-qua the Opossum, Di-li the Skunk, and Sa-lo-li the Squirrel, joined Raccoon and they spent their days making large clay pots to hold the water.

All the best fire builders, Terrapin, Eagle, and Yona the Bear, kept huge fires going day and night to dry the water pots. Beaver the dam builder offered to help them too.

Yona dragged in the logs and placed the kindling twigs. Eagle carried in coals from the central Fire and fanned the flames with his powerful wings. Beaver cut logs and branches with his sharp teeth. As for Terrapin the Doctor, he knew how to talk to Fire.

For days the fires blazed and the pots glowed red. One by one they were taken from the fire and allowed to cool. All the animals in the forest took pots filled with water to their homes. They covered the pots with woven mats and set them under what little shade remained from trees with dry, yellow leaves.

Before the river and all the streams dried away, the animals filled hundreds of pots with clean water, enough to last for months if they were careful. But months passed, and still no rain came. And the water in the pots was running low.

Terrapin called for another council to decide what could be done. It seemed that all the water on the earth had disappeared. Ji-Stu the Rabbit, known throughout the forest as the Messenger, carried the news of the council to all his neighbors.

At the council, Otter voted to move to another country and look for water there. Deer recommended chewing acorns, and Yona the Bear invited everyone to move to his winter home in the mountains, where springs of cold water run year round.

While the crowd considered Yona's offer, Ji-Stu the Rabbit jumped up suddenly and said, "There's water down deep in the ground. Terrapin told me, didn't you Terrapin?"

The big turtle walked toward the Fire and said, "Yes, Ji-Stu, that it true. There is water deep in the ground. But to reach it, we will all be forced to work hard for days and days. And we need to begin now, before all our water pots are empty!"

At daylight the next morning, Terrapin went out alone to find the right place to dig. He spoke to the earth and he spoke to the air, asking them to show him the way to the water.

"Let my feet know the way to go," Terrapin said, clearing his mind of all thoughts until his feet began to move.

Before long his feet stopped again, and he knew that he had found the best place in the forest to dig for water. He thrust his walking stick into the hard ground to mark the spot.

Terrapin called on all the best diggers, Groundhog and Otter, Crawdad and Ground Squirrel. They started digging a huge round hole, then everyone else joined in, digging with handmade tools, paddles, and sticks. Everyone, that is, except Ji-Stu the Rabbit.

While his neighbors worked away, Ji-Stu sat dozing in his little house by the dried-up riverbed. The others were so busy working that they did not notice his absence until lunchtime.

"Where's Ji-Stu?" Otter wanted to know. "I don't remember seeing him this morning, do any of you?"

"Well, if he had been here, we'd have all heard him bragging," grumbled Yona the Bear.

Everyone agreed that they had not heard Ji-Stu bragging about how digging the well was his idea. It was all he could talk about yesterday! Yona and Si-qua the Opossum decided to go and pay the lazy Ji-Stu a visit.

"Wait for me!" Otter yelled after them. He knew that if Ji-Stu the Rabbit was involved, something interesting was sure to happen, and he did not want to miss it.

"Ji-Stu!" Yona yelled through the rabbit's doorway. "If you want any of our water, you had better come and help us dig the well!"

Ji-Stu greeted his neighbors with a wide grin as he strolled out of his house. Then he stood up as tall as he could and sniffed.

"You should be thanking me for the privilege of digging the well yourselves. It was my idea, you know," he said proudly, then stamped back into his house.

"Ho!" Yona bellowed as loudly as he could. "You'll not have any of our water, you lazy rabbit!"

Sure enough, the animals dug their well deep into the earth until they reached an underground stream of icy, clean water. They all feasted and celebrated with a dance that evening. Ji-Stu heard the singing from across the valley and jumped out of bed at once. Why had he not been invited to the dance?!

Yona the Bear saw him coming down the path. "Go away, Ji-Stu! This feast is for those who work, not for those who sleep!"

Everyone else agreed, so Ji-Stu the Rabbit shrugged his shoulders and laughed, racing back toward his home. But he stopped laughing when the crowd could no longer hear him. Ji-Stu's own pots of water would soon be empty. Oh, how he wished it would rain.

Days passed, and one morning Ji-Stu awoke thirsty and hungry and dipped his drinking cup into his last water pot. It came back empty. This was the day Ji-Stu had dreaded for so long. His supply of water was totally gone.

Ji-Stu sat down and began to think. Maybe he could sneak down to the well the animals had built. Surely they would not notice if just a little water was missing.

He waited until well after sundown, covered his ears and shoulders with a dark hide, then slipped away into the night. He returned home with a pot of water big enough to last for several days. But when it was gone, there was still no sign of rain.

The thirsty Ji-Stu returned to the well again and again. No one was there late at night. He no longer even bothered to disguise himself.

"This is easy." Ji-Stu laughed to himself one night as he pulled a heavy pot of water from the well.

He laughed so hard that his stolen water sloshed over the side of the pot. Ji-Stu stepped in the muddy puddle without noticing it at all. Behind him, he left two perfect tracks that could only belong to Ji-Stu.

Yona the Bear stopped by the well the next day and noticed the footprints Ji-Stu had left behind. He leaned down and took a big sniff with his nose. Yona growled with anger and went off to find Terrapin.

"Ji-Stu the Rabbit is stealing our water," he told the big turtle. "What should we do, Terrapin?"

"He's coming to the well at night," said Terrapin. "That is the time to catch him. Take two of your neighbors and gather all the pine tar you can find. Bring it to me at the well."

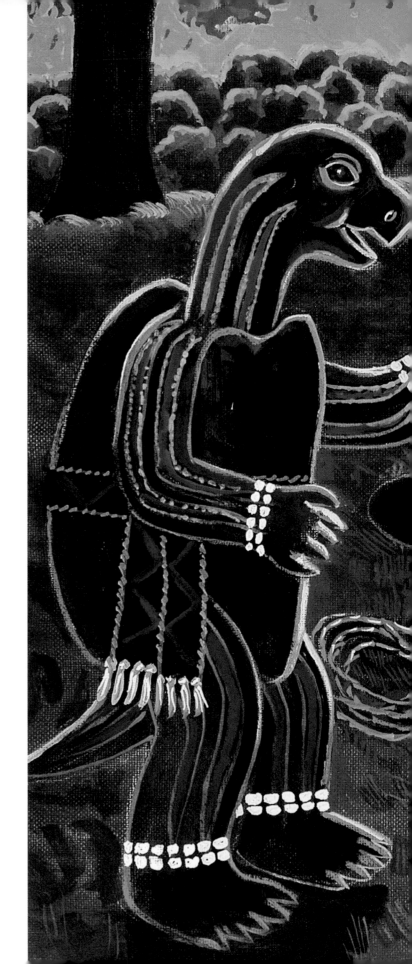

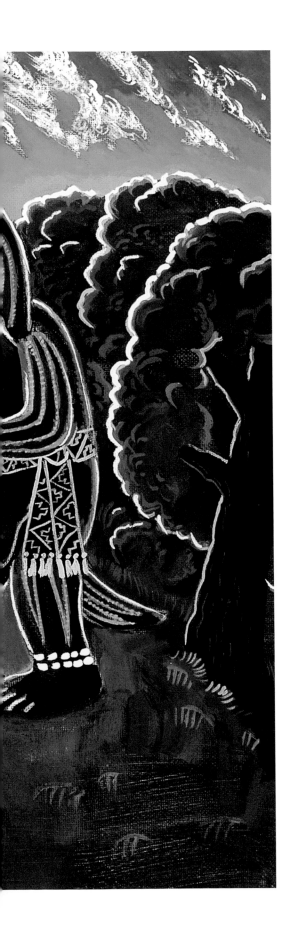

Yona found Otter and Si-qua the Opossum and the three of them carried empty gourds into the forest. A few hours later they set their gourds at Terrapin's feet. They were filled with sticky, yellow-brown pine tar.

Terrapin told Yona to drive a heavy post into the ground near the well. Terrapin then covered the post with pine tar, saying the right words to keep the tar from sticking to his hands. He shaped a face that looked like a wolf with acorn eyes, a black walnut nose, and tobacco leaf ears. Two leafy branches pushed through the tar made the creature's arms.

"What is this?" Yona asked in amazement. "How can this tar wolf help us to catch Ji-Stu? It cannot speak or move."

"That is exactly the reason it will catch him," Terrapin replied calmly. "Just you wait and see."

Back at his little house, Ji-Stu the Rabbit had just finished a nice hot bath with the last of his drinking water. He could afford such luxury now that getting fresh water had become so simple. He dried his ears and prepared for another trip to the well.

In the dim light of the stars, Ji-Stu skipped happily toward the well. But he stopped short and dropped his water pot when he saw a strange figure standing near the opening. This newcomer must be stealing water too!

"Who are you, and what are you doing here?" Ji-Stu demanded to know, but the tar wolf said not a word.

No matter how he tried, Ji-Stu could not make the stranger answer. Finally, he stood directly in front of the tar wolf, yelling, "If you don't answer me, I will kick you!" And that is what he did. Ji-Stu kicked the tar wolf as hard as he could. But something was wrong. The tar wolf was holding Ji-Stu's foot!

"Release me, or I will kick you again!" Ji-Stu screamed, and he kicked the tar wolf with his other foot.

Before Ji-Stu knew it, both his feet and both his hands were stuck fast to the tar wolf. He yelled until his throat hurt, but no one heard his cries for help. Ji-Stu looked down at his empty pot on the ground and wished for a drink of water.

The sound of voices made Ji-Stu open his eyes. Somehow he had managed to fall asleep, stuck as he was to the dreadful tar wolf! Yona the Bear whooped with delight when he caught sight of Ji-Stu, and even Terrapin had to chuckle.

"Oh look, Yona! Look, Terrapin!" Ji-Stu cried. "This thief tried to steal your water, and I have captured him!"

"Yes, the thief has certainly been captured!" Yona roared with laughter again as he and Terrapin turned to leave. "Now don't you let him get away, Ji-Stu!"

In all his years, poor Ji-Stu had never felt so helpless. Maybe he would stay stuck to this ugly tar wolf forever! Maybe he would starve or die of thirst right here beside the water well.

"Here, Ji-Stu, try this," said a familiar voice. It was Otter! "I use this oil to waterproof my coat. You'll be free in no time."

Otter poured the oil onto Ji-Stu's hands and feet, and sure enough they slipped right out of the gooey tar. Then he sat back happily to hear Ji-Stu's story about his battle with the evil tar wolf. Just as Ji-Stu was bragging to Otter that he would never steal from his neighbors again, a loud clap of thunder shook the ground. And while Ji-Stu made his promise, the rain began to fall.